OLIVER

Who Was Small But Mighty

For Nick, with love and thanks – MB
For Stephanie and John with love – NM

First published in paperback 2009 by Hodder Children's Books

Text copyright © Mara Bergman 2008
Illustration copyright © Nick Maland 2008

Hodder Children's Books
338 Euston Road, London NW1 3BH

Hodder Children's Books Australia
Level 17/207 Kent Street, Sydney, NSW 2000

The right of Mara Bergman to be identified as the author and Nick Maland as the illustrator of this
Work has been asserted by them in accordance with the Copyright, Designs and Patents Act 1988.

A catalogue record of this book is available from the British Library.

PB: 978 0340 93055 7
10 9 8 7 6 5

Printed in China

Hodder Children's Books is a division of Hachette Children's Books, an Hachette UK Company
www.hachette.co.uk

OLIVER

Who Was Small But Mighty

MARA BERGMAN * NICK MALAND

The night the wind started to bump and to bash
was the night the rain started to thump and to thrash.
Oliver was small, he didn't like it at all.
He wished he was tall and mighty.

But his boat was already waiting.

And what of the deep blue sea? Well...

it was certainly frothy

and certainly wild

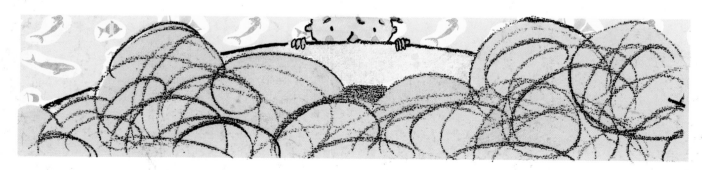

and a little bit scary
for one frightened child, but...

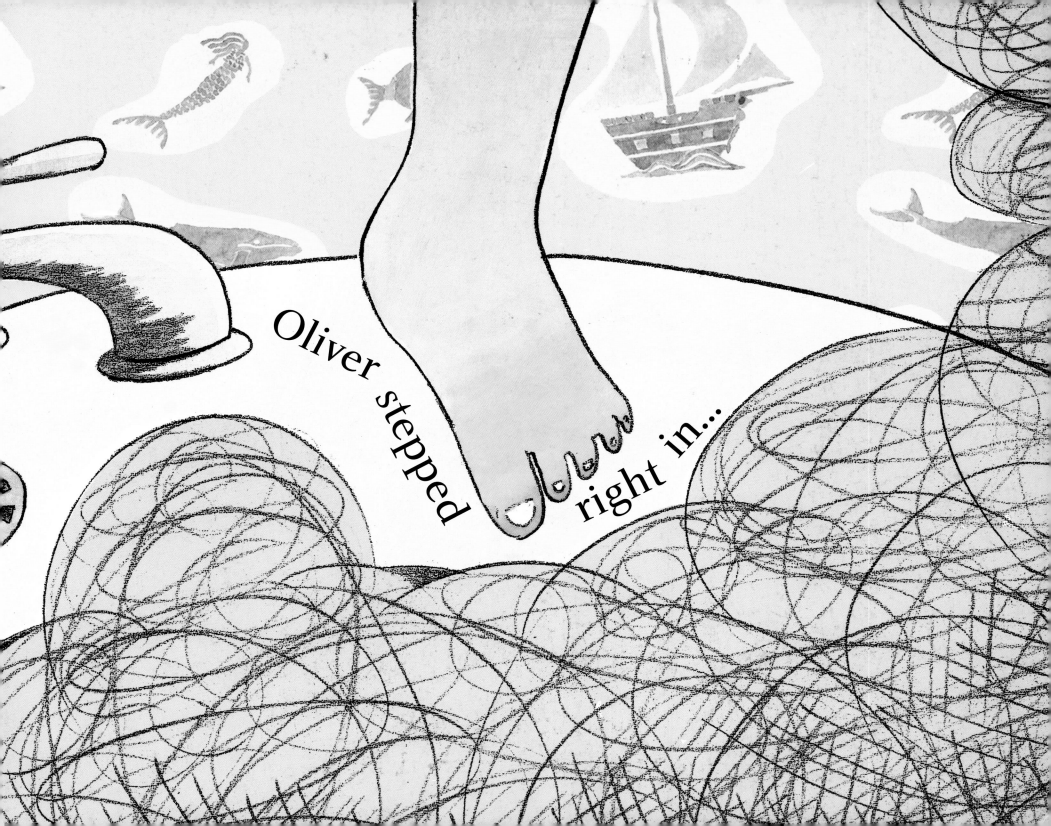

Oliver stepped right in...

and straight away set sail.

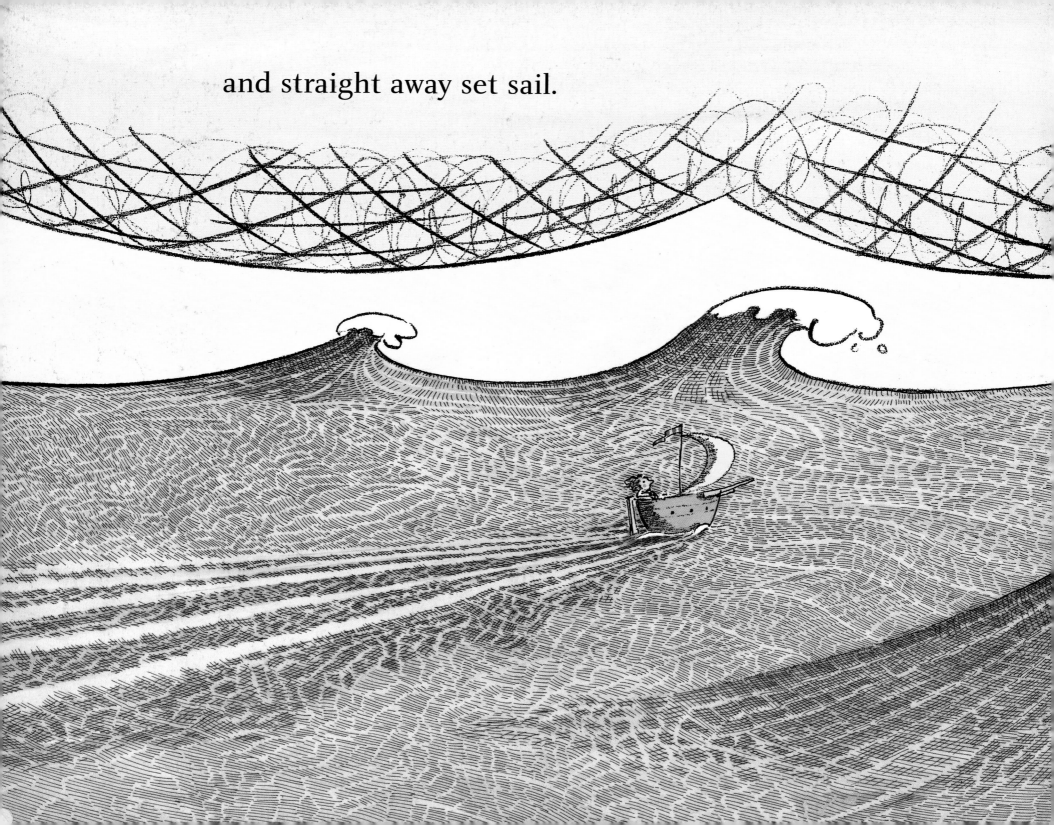

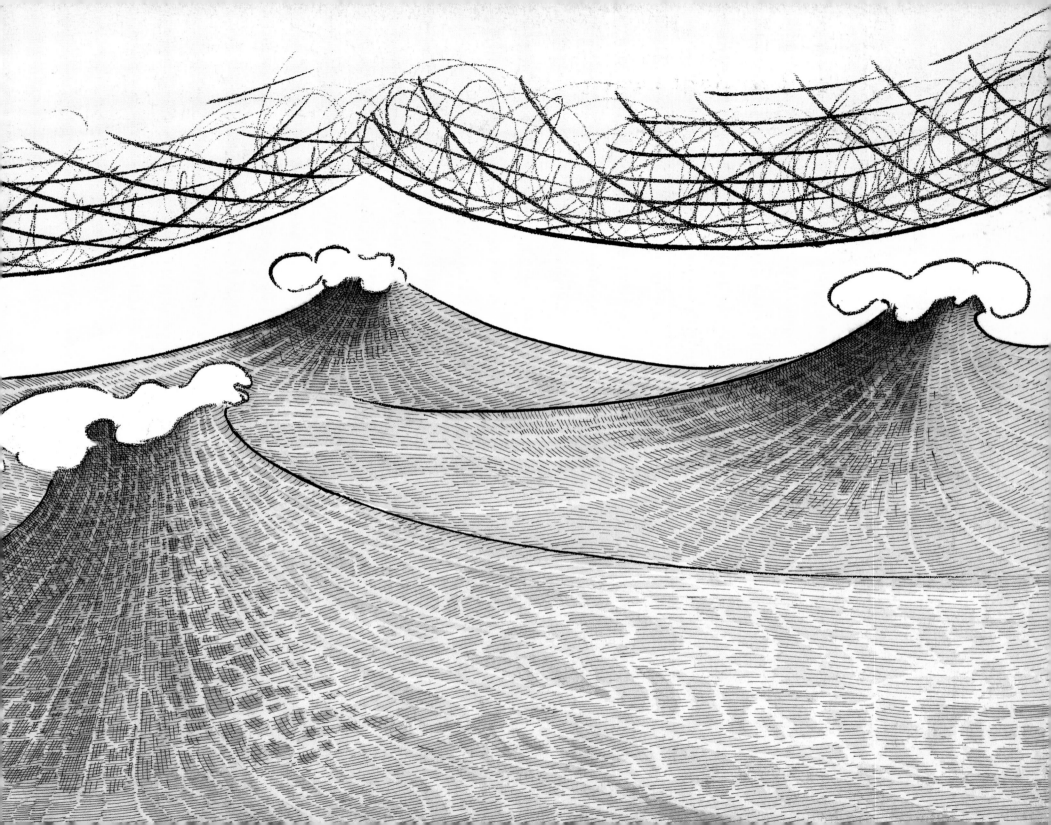

The fishes were swishing
and the fishes were swarming
when the seahorses came
and a group started forming...

of porpoises, seals, dolphins, mermaids and eels
and from a short distance...

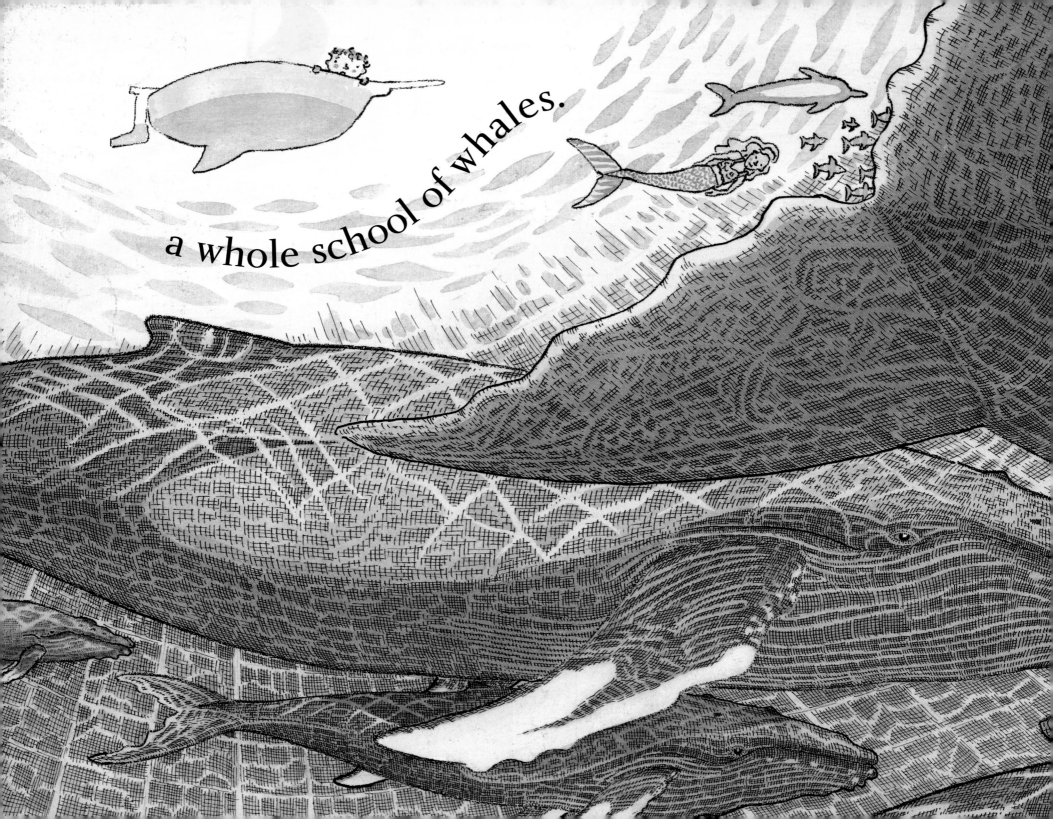

a whole school of whales.

Oliver was small,
he didn't like it at all.
He wished he was tall and mighty.

It turned out, the whales
were quite friendly.
With their giant tails splashing
that set the waves flashing...

they had Oliver
laughing and
laughing...

and laughing.

Oliver could have
stayed forever

but somehow he knew...

he had places to go
and things to do.
So he set sail again.

The winds were growing high
as some pirates came by
with their peg legs, tattoos,
missing teeth and wrecked shoes.

Some were bald,
some were hairy,
every one of them was scary
and demanded,
'Hand over your gold!'

Oliver was small,
he didn't like them at all.
He longed to be
tall and mighty.

But he dashed out

and thrashed out

and altogether lashed out

and frightened those
pirates away.

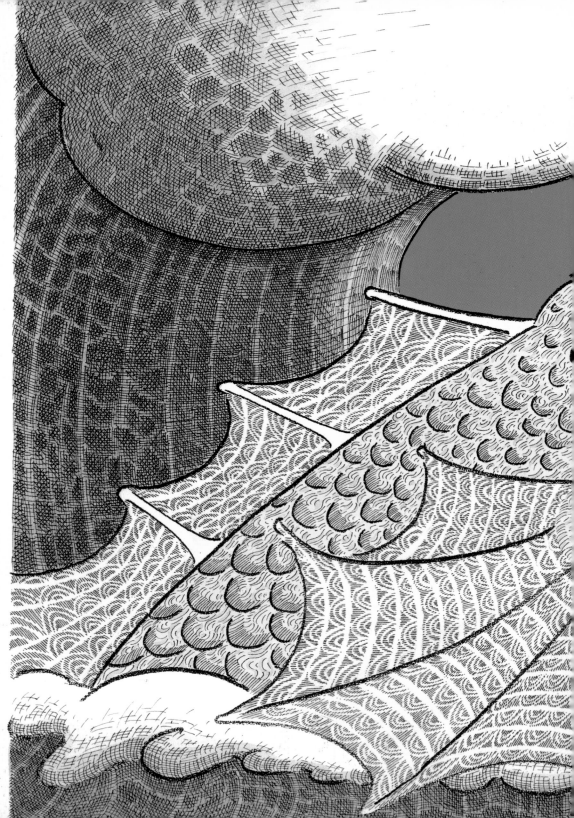

Now in the distance
Oliver could see
long sandy beaches
and swaying palm trees,
when suddenly—

The sea grew rougher and rougher.
The sailing grew tougher and tougher.
A thunderous **roar**
came near and **roared more!**

Oliver was small but for once and for all
he stood very tall and was **mighty!**
He cried out, he bellowed,
he kicked, screamed and yelled...

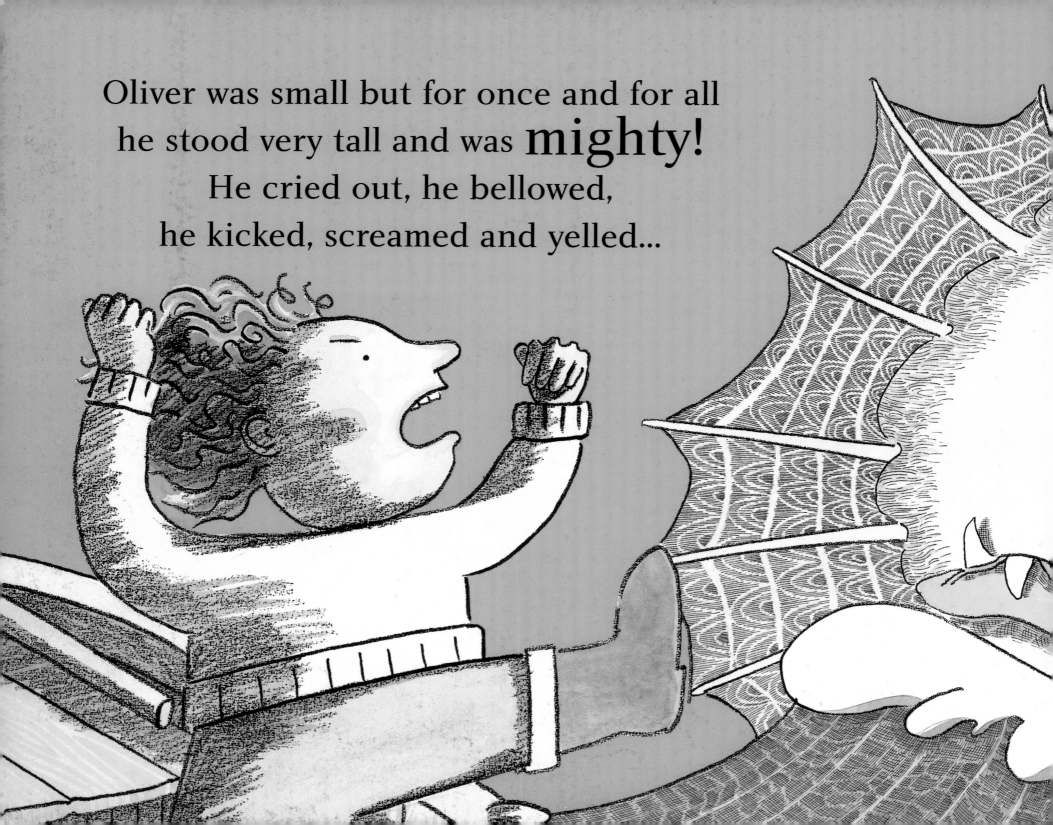

and he frightened
that monster away!

The sea grew calm,
the day grew still.

Shadows were creeping
over the hill...

It was Oliver's mum who snapped Oliver up,
and Oliver's dad who wrapped Oliver up.

Dry and rosy,

cuddly and cosy,

snugly and dozy,

Oliver set sail...

for sleep.